ROOSEVELT BANKS

Good-Kid-in-Training

ROOSEVELT BANKS

Good-Kid-in-Training

Laurie Calkhoven

with illustrations by Debbie Palen

ONE ELM
BOOKS

Egremont, Massachusetts

One Elm Books is an imprint of Red Chair Press LLC

Red Chair Press LLC   PO Box 333   South Egremont, MA 01258-0333

www.redchairpress.com

www.oneelmbooks.com

Publisher's Cataloging-In-Publication Data
Names: Calkhoven, Laurie, author. | Palen, Debbie, illustrator.
Title: Roosevelt Banks : Good-Kid-In-Training / Laurie Calkhoven ; with
    illustrations by Debbie Palen.

Description: [South Egremont, Massachusetts] : One Elm Books, an imprint
    of Red Chair Press LLC, [2020] | Summary: "When ten-year-old Roosevelt
    Banks discovers that his two best friends are planning a bike & camping
    trip, he wants more than anything to go along. There's just one
    problem--he doesn't have a bike. Roosevelt's parents agree to buy him a
    new bike IF he can manage to be good for two whole weeks. How can
    Roosevelt be good and be the same fun guy his friends want on the
    camping trip?"--Provided by publisher.

Identifiers: ISBN 9781947159181 (library hardcover) | ISBN 9781947159198
    (paperback) |ISBN 9781947159204 (ebook PDF)

Subjects: LCSH: Boys--Conduct of life--Juvenile fiction. | Friendship--
    Juvenile fiction. | Bicycles--Juvenile fiction. | Camping--Juvenile
    fiction. | CYAC: Conduct of life--Fiction. | Friendship--Fiction. |
    Bicycles--Fiction. | Camping--Fiction.

Classification: LCC PZ7.C12878 Ro 2020 (print) | LCC PZ7.C12878 (ebook) |
    DDC [Fic]--dc23

LC record available at https://lccn.loc.gov/2019934117

Main body text set in 17/24 Baskerville

Printed in Canada

619 1P S20FN

For the good kids in my life
—Logan, Bennett, and Madison

CHAPTER ONE

Listen, Roosevelt

So far it was a regular Monday.

Tommy and I burped during silent reading time and made the whole class laugh.

At recess I squatted down really fast while Josh ripped a piece of paper and made everyone think I had split my pants. *Fake out!*

All three of us smeared ketchup on our mouths after lunch and lurched around after the girls like zombies. Emily Park screamed!

Now it was time for some real fun. I jumped off the school bus and zoomed down the hill to the creek. I teetered on the edge for a second and then popped onto a rock in the middle of the water. Safe! Tommy and Josh were right behind me.

"Want to meet back here and hunt frogs?" I asked.

The three of us hung out almost every day after school. We were the only three best friends in fourth grade. All the other best friends came in pairs.

Josh and Tommy didn't answer.

"Frogs?" I asked again.

Josh's eyes slid sideways toward Tommy.

Tommy's eyes slid sideways toward Josh.

I came up with a new idea. "If Mrs. Crabapple isn't home we can slither through her yard and spy on Tommy's brothers. Maybe they'll start talking about what girls they like again—*gross!*"

Crabby old Mrs. Crawford doesn't like kids in her yard for any reason. Not for slithering. Not for running after balls. And especially not for petting the rabbits she keeps in a hutch in her backyard.

Now Josh's eyes blinked at Tommy.

Tommy's eyes stared at his sneakers.

Neither one of them said a word. That was definitely weird.

"What do you want to do?" I asked.

"Can't hang out today, Roosevelt," Josh mumbled. "I have to ride my bike."

"Me, too," Tommy said. He scuffed the toe of his sneaker in the mud on the creek bank. "I have to ride my bike."

"*Have to?* What do you mean *have to?* Nobody *has* to ride a bike." I didn't have a bike. Not anymore. And they both knew it.

Now Josh and Tommy's eyes started acting even weirder. Their eyeballs darted up, down, and sideways. They blinked like crazy.

"What's going on?" I asked. "Why don't you want to do something we can do together?"

Finally Josh's eyeballs looked right into mine. "Listen, Roosevelt," he said.

Sentences that start with 'Listen, Roosevelt' never end with something good. But usually it's Mom or Dad or a teacher saying, 'Listen, Roosevelt,' not one of my two best friends.

"My dad's taking me and two of my friends on a bicycle trip. We're going to bike all the way to the state park on the old railroad trail. And camp. It's for the three-day weekend next month," Josh said, all in a rush. "He told me last night. He said you and Tommy could come, but you don't have a bike."

"Josh called me on my cell phone last night," Tommy said, still staring at his sneakers.

Cell phone. Another thing they had that I didn't.

"My parents already said I could go," Tommy added.

I started to feel like the rock I was standing on was sinking into the creek bed and I was sinking along with it.

"He said you could bring two friends. Who's taking my place?" I asked.

Josh's ears turned red. "I don't know yet."

I thought of reasons why they couldn't go. "How are you going to get camping stuff there on your bikes?" I asked.

4

"My dad has a trailer thing that attaches to the back of his bike," Josh said. "He can bring everything. The tent. The food. The sleeping bags. The fishing poles."

Tommy's eyes flashed. "We're going fishing? Awesome."

Josh raised his hand for a high five. *Slap!*

"We'll tell ghost stories around the campfire," he said. *Slap.*

"And roast marshmallows," Tommy added. *Slap.*

"And swim in the lake." *Slap.*

"And not take showers or wash our hair for three days." *Slap.*

"And pee in the woods." *Slap.*

Each high five made me feel worse and worse. I wanted to pee in the woods, too.

"Maybe we'll see a bear." *Slap.*

Tommy cracked up. "But not while we're peeing!" *Slap.*

"My dad's gonna love it!" Josh said. "I bet he even

moves closer to me so we can go all the time."

Oh, great, I thought, *so they can go on even more fun trips without me.*

"Why can't you tell your dad to plan a trip without bikes? Just plain camping?" I asked.

A flicker of surprise crossed Josh's face, like he never even thought about how he could include me. "My dad just got a new bike," he said. "It was his idea."

"You can't ride your bikes all the way to the state park," I told them. "It's too far. You'll keel over and die and a bear will eat you." Okay, maybe I didn't say it. Maybe I was yelling.

"We will too make it," Josh said. "We're gonna ride our bikes every day after school. And Saturdays and Sundays, too."

"It's thirty miles," Tommy said quietly. "We have to train to get ready."

"You can't bike thirty miles," I yelled.

"Can, too!" Josh yelled back. "We're gonna work

our way up. We're BDTs, bike-dudes-in-training," Josh said.

BDTs? They already have a secret nickname?

"You know I'd invite you if you had a bike, Roosevelt," Josh said. His voice trailed off.

I was starting to think that was a big lie. "You're the reason I don't have a bike anymore," I yelled.

"That experiment was your idea," Josh yelled back. "It wasn't my fault."

"If you were really my friend, you'd tell your dad you didn't want to go without me," I said.

"If you were really *my* friend, you'd be happy my dad was taking me on this cool trip."

Tommy's eyes darted from me to Josh and back to me. He looked sorry, but not sorry enough to skip the trip. "I'd let you borrow Dante and Malik's bike," he said, "but they took it apart to make a Ferris wheel for their gerbil. Maybe you can ask your parents for a new bike," Tommy said. He turned to Josh. "Wouldn't that be cool?"

Josh shrugged. He was still mad. "I guess," he said.

"Will you ask them?" Tommy asked me.

I didn't trust myself to say yes without maybe sounding like I was about to cry—not that I was, there was something in my throat—so I only nodded.

"It would be awesome if you could come," Tommy said. He turned back to Josh. "Wouldn't it?"

"I guess I can wait to ask someone else," Josh mumbled.

I wasn't so sure my parents would say yes to a new bike. They were steamed when my bike got broken. And even though Tommy was trying to find a way to include me, Josh was ready to put another kid in my place. He and Tommy were going to be BDTs every day after school and on the weekends. I'd be alone.

What if Tommy and Josh replace me with a new best friend?

That's what I was thinking when Tommy pointed and shouted. "Frog!"

I spun on my heel to look, forgetting that I was on

a slippery rock. The next thing I knew I was ankle-deep in creek water. *Splash!*

CHAPTER TWO
Sploosh, Squeak

I slammed the front door and threw my backpack down with a thud. Our border collie, Millard Fillmore, should have been waiting for me and wagging his tail. He wasn't.

My mother looked up from her computer in the corner of the living room. "Welcome home, sunshine," she said. "How was school?"

"Horrible," I said.

"What's wrong?" she asked.

"Nothing."

"Mrs. Anderson didn't call. Did she send you home with a note?"

"No," I said.

"What about Principal Esposito?"

"I'm not in trouble." *Geez, a guy can't win, even at home.*

"Did something happen?" Mom asked.

"No," I said.

"Okay." Mom took a big breath. Parents and teachers do that—a lot. I guess when you're old you need extra air.

"Do you have any homework?" she asked.

"Just my stupid story," I answered.

"I thought you liked your story."

"Not anymore," I said.

"Why don't you think about how you can fix it while you have your snack. Then you can change clothes and go play."

"I don't have anyone to hang out with," I said, stomping toward the kitchen. Except because my shoes and socks were filled with creek water, my stomping was really splooshing and squeaking.

I *splooshed, squeaked, splooshed, squeaked* across the living room.

"Roosevelt Theodore Banks," Mom said.

If anyone ever wondered which President Roosevelt I was named after, all they had to do was wait for my mom to get mad at me.

"I thought we agreed you were only going to wear your old sneakers in the creek. Now your new ones will smell, too."

"It was an accident," I said.

"You *accidentally* jumped in the creek?" Mom asked.

You'd think that at least a guy's mom would believe him, even if his two best friends were traitors who planned cool bicycle trips without him.

Mom's computer pinged and she took another big old person's breath. "I'll talk to you about it when I finish up here."

I *splooshed, squeaked* on my way to the kitchen.

"Take your shoes off!" Mom yelled.

When I finally got to the kitchen after all that stuff, Millard Fillmore was sitting at my four-year-old

sister Kennedy's feet. Millard Fillmore's eyes were trained on the cookie she was trying to feed to a doll. He thumped his tail when he saw me, but he didn't move.

"Another traitor," I muttered. But Fillmore doesn't speak human, so his tail only thumped harder. I scratched his head for a second.

"Rosie want tea?" Kennedy asked, raising her blue-and-white teapot.

"*Roosevelt* is a boy and doesn't play tea party," I snapped. That wasn't true. Sometimes I did when no one was looking, but not today.

Kennedy's lower lip started to tremble. Mom would be really mad if I made Kennedy cry. Plus I felt a little bad. She's just a kid.

"Dolly wants tea," I said, pointing to her doll.

That was enough to make her happy. Kennedy poured pretend tea into little blue cups. Too bad nothing that small could cheer me up.

CHAPTER THREE

Smash Your Face, Not Your Brains

Oatmeal chocolate chip cookies and milk didn't make me feel better. Neither did lots of licks from Fillmore. While Kennedy chattered about dolls and preschool drama, I thought about how much fun I'd be missing while the BDTs rode their bikes.

I escaped from the kitchen before Mom could come and talk things over. Upstairs, I made sure to blow my breath out when I walked past the door to the Attic of Doom. Tommy's older brothers Dante and Malik told us that ghosts can slip into your body while you're breathing in. And late at night when everyone's sleeping I can hear ghost noises coming from up there.

The first thing I did when I got to my room was check my bank. Maybe I could buy my own bike. I had only $1.47. I guess I shouldn't have bought that exploding volcano kit for $14.95, especially since it made a huge mess in the kitchen and got all over Kennedy.

If I looked out the window, I'd see Tommy pedaling toward Josh's. Instead I sat at my desk and looked at the story I was writing for school. It was about three best friends who discover they have super powers. One has super smarts (that would be me), one has super strength (that would be Josh), and one has ESP and can read minds (that would be Tommy). But now I didn't feel like finishing. I pushed it aside and started a new story.

TRAITORS
by Roosevelt Banks

One day, two boys named Josh and Tommy sneak away on a bike trip without their best friend Lincoln.

The traitors run into a bear on the old railroad trail. The bear roars and snaps its teeth. It's a hungry bear and Josh and Tommy will make a tasty meal— even if they are traitors.

The boys scream. "Help! Help! We're going to be bear food!"

Lincoln has super hearing. He can hear his ex-friends' screams from miles away. He knows Josh and Tommy can't out run a hungry bear, but Lincoln has a secret. It's a magic jet pack. He uses it to fly to their rescue, even though they don't deserve it.

When Lincoln gets there—seconds later—the bear has Josh in one hand and Tommy in the other. He is deciding which head to chomp off first with his big bear teeth when Lincoln flies by and kicks that bear in the face.

The bear is so surprised he drops Josh and Tommy. He swats at Lincoln, but Lincoln dances away in the air before bravely coming in for another kick and another.

Josh and Tommy huddle on the ground, too scared to run.

"Get moving, boys!" Lincoln yells. "Hop on your bikes and race away."

That gives them the push they need. As soon as Lincoln sees his ex-friends are safe, he flies home. An hour later, they knock on his door.

"You saved our lives!" Tommy exclaims.

"We were bear food for sure until you came along," Josh says. "You're the bravest person I know."

Tommy gives Lincoln a high-five. "We're sorry we left you out. We'll never do it again. Will you forgive us?"

"You're our best friend—and our hero," Josh adds.

Lincoln forgives his friends and gives them each their own jet pack so they can all fly together, because that's the kind of good guy he is.

The End

I wrote really fast and it was messy, but it was a great story. I started over at the beginning, neater this time, and added cool details like blood and guts dripping from the bear's teeth from his most recent meal and beads of sweat on Josh's and Tommy's foreheads. It was A+ work.

I sat back and put my feet up, feeling a little better. On the bulletin board above my desk was a picture of Josh, Tommy, and me each holding a blue ribbon we had won at the Science Fair. Next to it were pictures of my bike at the bottom of the big hill on Third Street with a partly smashed melon wearing my bike helmet. In another picture, a melon head with no helmet was smashed into a million pieces with melon brains all over the street. The front bike wheel was bent, too.

We proved that it's better to crash your bike wearing a helmet. We made a big sign that said:

Wear a helmet.
Smash your face, not your brains.

Josh's father planned a bike trip after my broken bike won Josh a blue ribbon. That was not fair. And it wasn't fair that Tommy said he would go without me.

Plus I never even got a reward for thinking up my excellent idea. Instead I got called Roosevelt Theodore Banks a whole bunch of times by Mom and Dad for breaking my bike. You'd think it was people heads that got smashed, not melon faces.

I went back to my story. I was drawing a picture of a humongous bear with Josh in one hand and Tommy in the other when Mom came to see me. She read my new story and asked if it had anything to do with how upset I was.

Mom likes words like *upset* when there are much better words to use. Words like *angry* and *boiling mad* and *super pissed off.* I'm not allowed to say that last one out loud, but I was thinking it inside my head.

"Josh and Tommy are going on a bicycle trip without me. And they're going to be bike-dudes-in-training and they're going to put some other kid in my place, or become two best friends instead of three," I said.

Mom felt sad with me for a few minutes. Then she said all kinds of junk that moms have to say. Junk about how Josh and Tommy would be busy, but that didn't mean they didn't want to be friends anymore.

Yeah, but they'll have all kinds of secret jokes and stories and cool things to talk about and I'll be left out.

Junk about how she'd set up some play dates for after school and Saturdays.

Hello? I'm ten. I don't play. I hang out.

Junk about how I have a sister and so I always have someone to play with.

Yeah, but baby, girly games.

Junk about taking something bad and turning it into something good.

Yeah, like a new bike!

I hoped Mom would come up with the idea of a new bike all by herself, but she didn't. Mom was super quick to say no to things, especially to things that cost money, so I didn't ask.

But Dad was different. Maybe if I was really sad when I told him my troubles, he'd tell Mom I needed a new bike—a super-fast racing bike.

The whole thing would be easier than finding fireworks on the Fourth of July.

CHAPTER FOUR
The Dust Bowl

I slipped into the garage so I could catch Dad the minute he got home. But he was already there. He liked to sit in his car to grade papers. He said he didn't get enough quiet at home, and his college students—he's an American History professor—liked to hang out in his office when he was there.

"Hey, buddy," Dad said when he saw me. He had a stack of papers on his lap. The one on top said, THE DUST BOWL.

"Who'd want a bowl of dust?" I asked.

"It's not that kind of bowl," he said.

"Is it a football game, like the Super Bowl?"

"Not that kind of bowl either. It's about a time in the 1930s when it didn't rain for a long, long time in the middle of the country. There was a bad drought and the crops died. It was during the Great Depression."

"Samantha Guerrero's mother has depression. She takes pills."

"Well, in Samantha's mother's case, depression means she's very sad."

I remembered why I was there in the first place. "I have depression," I said. "I'm very, very sad, and maybe a little mad, too."

"You're sad?" Dad asked. "Sad and mad? Must be pretty serious."

"It is," I told him. "I'm about to lose my two best friends. All because I don't have a bike."

I thought telling Dad my sad tale would make him come up with the idea of buying me a new bike all on his own over a delicious dinner of spaghetti and meatballs. But dinner turned out to be nothing like what I expected.

In the first place, we didn't have spaghetti and

meatballs. We had—*blechety blech*—turkey meatloaf and lima beans and mashed potatoes. Everyone knows mashed potatoes are only good when there's corn to mix in with them to cover the potato taste. And there is nothing, not one thing, that can ever cover the taste of lima beans. Even Millard Fillmore won't eat them, and he eats everything. Even dirty socks.

That's dog Fillmore, not President Fillmore. I don't know what President Fillmore ate. Probably not socks or lima beans.

Thank goodness for ketchup, or I would have been in real trouble.

In the second place, while I did my best to eat every bite of my *blechety blech* dinner like a shining star and didn't say *blechety blech blech* out loud even once, Dad never brought up the idea of getting me a new bike.

I waited and waited and waited.

I tried to lock our brains together, thinking *new bike, new bike, new bike.*

Then I waited some more. *New bike, new bike.*

I waited through Kennedy's story about who got a three-minute timeout at preschool. No surprise—it wasn't her. I waited through Dad's even longer story about a dude who fell asleep in class and started snoring. I waited through Mom's story about Aunt Jessica's new baby and how cute it is even though it has a squished up face in every single picture I've seen. And I didn't even mention the smell that came out of its diaper when we went to visit.

I waited through every single *blechety blech* bite. No one told a story about how I should get a new bike.

And then I was done waiting.

"I should get a new bike so that I can go on the bike trip with Josh and Tommy. And I should get it tomorrow so that I can be a bike-dude-in-training with them, or I'll fall behind and die on the way to the state park and get eaten by a bear."

Now Dad was suddenly all willing to lock brains with someone—only it was Mom, not me. They looked at each other and then at me. They had turned into one giant blob of Super Parent.

"Whose idea was it to send a bike down the big hill for your science fair experiment?" Mom asked.

"Mine," I muttered.

"And who volunteered to use *your* bike?" Dad asked. "Without permission."

I crossed my arms over my chest. "Me."

"And who sent your bike crashing down the big hill with melons tied to the handlebars?" Dad asked.

"It was a really old bike," I said. "My legs were getting too long for it. If I kept riding that bike, I would have had an accident. My knees could have knocked me in the chin. I would have gone flying off and smashed my face." I gave them both my most serious, grown-up look. "But not my brains, because I always wear a helmet. Like you taught me."

"Roosevelt," Dad said. "You can't destroy a perfectly good bicycle because you want a new one."

"I saved lives, people. I saved lives! No kid in my

school is going to ride a bike without a helmet after seeing those smashed up melon heads."

"Melon heads," Kennedy repeated with a nod.

"Shouldn't I get a reward for winning the science fair and for saving lives?" I asked. "My birthday is coming in four months and three weeks and six days. It could be an early birthday present."

"We were going to give your bike to Kennedy when she got bigger," Mom said. "Maybe your birthday present should be a new bike for your sister."

"What???????????"

I clamped my lips together to keep any madder-than-mad words from spilling out and getting me into bigger-than-big trouble.

I guess my face was talking for me, because Dad said, "Want to be excused, buddy?"

And I hadn't even choked down one lima bean yet.

I was out of there before he even finished asking the question. I ran to my room, slammed the door, and threw myself onto the bed. All I could think was *no more best friends for me.*

CHAPTER FIVE
Good-Kid-in-Training

I lay on my bed listening to the cleaning-up-from-dinner noises. Then came the getting-Kennedy-ready-for-bed noises and big, smoochy kisses as she passed by my door.

I didn't hear any let's-go-see-Roosevelt-and-cheer-him-up-with-a-new-bike noises.

Finally, after hours and hours and hours, there was a knock on my door.

"Come in," I said. Only it sounded like *comb in* because my nose was all full of snot. Not from crying. I must have caught a cold.

Mom sat on my bed. Dad pulled up the desk chair, which would be way more fun to sit in if it was on wheels and spun around. Just saying.

"I guess you feel pretty bad," Mom said.

I nodded and tried to make myself look extra pitiful.

She brushed the hair off my forehead. "Maybe you can still join your friends for the camping trip, even if you can't bike there and back with them."

"How?" I asked.

"We can drive you to the campground," she said.

"You'll be there for the best part," Dad added. "Think of all the hard work Josh and Tommy will have to do, and you get to show up just in time for the fun."

"Josh won't say yes to that," I said. "He wants another BDT on the trip."

"BDT?" Mom asked.

"Bike-dude-in-training," I answered. "And besides, Josh and Tommy will be riding their bikes every single day to get ready, and I won't have anyone to hang out with."

Then I made an even better argument. "It's not

fair that Josh's dad is taking him and Tommy on a bike trip after what happened to my bike. It's not fair. You should call and tell him that."

"I know it feels that way," Dad said. "But Josh's father doesn't live with him and Josh's mom. He may not even know about the science fair."

"Tommy shouldn't go. He was my best friend for a long time before Josh moved into the neighborhood. He should have told Josh he wouldn't go on any trip unless I could go, too."

"Roosevelt," Mom said. "Do you want Tommy to miss out on a fun trip because you can't go?"

I slumped against my pillows. I knew she wanted me to say, 'No,' but I didn't want to.

"Buddy, the truth is that it was *your* decision to send *your* bike crashing down that hill. Not Josh's. And not Tommy's," Dad said.

I pretended I was thinking about what he said, but I still thought I was right.

"You should have asked for permission before you

did your experiment. But we are proud of you for coming up with such a good idea for the science fair," Dad said.

"And for saving lives," Mom added. Her lips were twitching like she was trying not to laugh, so I'm not sure she meant it. Not really.

Then they did their Parent Mind Meld again.

"We've talked it over," Dad said.

I sat up. Was I getting a new bike?

"IF you can stay out of trouble for the next two weeks—that means being good at school, helping out with Kennedy, and doing your chores without being told—and IF we can find a good secondhand bike at a yard sale, then you can go on the bike trip with your friends."

I eyed Mom. "Really?"

"Really," she said. "But you have to stay out of trouble. No trouble at home and no trouble at school."

"Easy peasy," I said, giving her a hug. Moms like

junk like hugs and kisses. Then I slapped Dad the biggest high-five ever. A new bike!

I couldn't wait to tell Josh and Tommy. I was going on the bike trip!

CHAPTER SIX

Totally Impossible

I told Josh and Tommy the good news at the bus stop the next morning. They were P-S-Y-C-H-E-D psyched.

"Awesome," Josh said, giving me a high-five.

"Cool," Tommy said. "It'll be more fun if you come with us."

The bus pulled up and we got on. Eddie Spaghetti grunted at me like a zombie when I dropped into the seat next to him. His name's not really Spaghetti, but once in second grade he laughed so hard at lunch that a spaghetti noodle shot out of his nose. It was the most awesomest thing ever.

Our moms used to work together at the college, before my mom started teaching online classes at home. He doesn't have a fourth-grade best friend, but everyone likes him. He bounces from group to group.

"When are you getting it?" Tommy asked. "Can you ride with us after school?"

"Getting what?" Eddie said.

"A new bike," I told him, "so I can go on a bike-camping trip with Josh and his dad and Tommy."

"He said I could bring two friends," Josh added.

"But I have to wait two weeks to get my bike. So I can't ride today," I told them.

"Two weeks?" Josh asked.

"Yeah, my parents want me to stay out of trouble for two weeks and help Kennedy and do my homework and chores and junk like that. And then I get a new bike."

"Dude, stay out of trouble for two weeks?" Eddie laughed, but it wasn't a funny laugh—it was kind of mean. "You?"

I looked at Josh and Tommy for support. All four

of their eyebrows were pointing way up, like they thought it was impossible, too.

"Totally impossible," Eddie said. He leaned forward and talked to Josh. "Give it up, man. Invite someone else on your bike trip."

"Nothing's impossible," I told them. "I'm getting that new bike."

For the rest of the ride to school Eddie was asking Josh questions about the bike trip like I wasn't even there. He kept talking about his own bike like he wanted to go.

I started to worry. Was Eddie right? Was it impossible for me to stay out of trouble for two whole weeks? And would Eddie bounce his way into my spot on the bike trip?

I thought hard about being good all day in school. I didn't whisper jokes to the kids around me during silent reading time. I didn't sing loud and off-key during music to crack everybody up. And at lunch I especially didn't flick the crust of my bread at Eddie

Spaghetti after he flicked his at me. I even raised my hand during math and volunteered to do a problem on the whiteboard. Okay, so I got it wrong. I still raised my hand.

Let me tell you, being good is H-A-R-D hard. How was I going to keep it up for two whole weeks?

After school, Millard Fillmore greeted me at my door with his wagging tail. I buried my face in his fur and breathed deep, smelling his doggie smell.

"Hi, Mom," I said. "I was good all day in school and I came straight home and didn't fall in the creek or get in any trouble."

"Great, buddy," Mom said. "One day down, thirteen to go."

Uh-oh, thirteen is definitely not a lucky number.

CHAPTER SEVEN

The Super Boring Life of a Good Kid

For the next few days I was good in school and good at home. I even took a walk around the backyard and picked up all the dried-out Fillmore poop so Dad could mow the lawn. Twice at recess I didn't play soccer with the guys because I knew Eddie Spaghetti was planning to kick the ball over the fence into the woods on the other side.

We had been told not to climb the fence, but that didn't mean it wasn't a fun thing to do. We had races to see who could reach the top, jump down to the other side, grab the ball, and make it back before the recess monitor noticed. If you got caught, looking for the soccer ball was the perfect excuse for climbing the fence. But I couldn't risk it. I had a new bike on the line.

So recess was totally boring, and the bus rides were even worse. All Josh and Tommy could talk about was how far they had biked the day before and how far they were going to bike after school that day.

And Eddie Spaghetti was totally trying to noodle his way into my spot on the trip.

"Do you think you'll be able to keep up, Roosevelt?" he asked really loud. "Even if by some miracle you get your bike, Josh and Tommy will be training for two weeks without you."

Before I could protest he leaned forward and spoke to Josh. "*I* ride *my* bike every day after school."

"I will too keep up," I muttered, but I'm not sure Josh was listening.

I ran up to Josh and Tommy at the end of recess that day. Eddie was glued to Josh's side and they shut up really fast, like they were talking about me. Josh's ears turned red. Eddie pretended to smile at me, but it was more like a smirk.

Tommy and I had been best friends since we were three, long before Josh moved into the neighborhood. I cornered him in front of the tater tots on the lunch line and got him to tell me what was going on.

"Eddie really wants to go on the bike trip," Tommy said. "But Josh's dad told him he could only bring two friends. He says four boys are way too much for him to handle."

"Josh told Eddie I'm going, right?" I asked. "I'm going to get that new bike."

"That's what Josh said," Tommy said. "But Eddie said it would be cooler for everybody, especially Josh's dad, if someone fun went along."

"Someone fun?" I asked. "Is Eddie more fun than me?"

"Josh won't go back on his word," Tommy said.

But he didn't answer the question about Eddie being more fun than me.

I looked over at our lunch table to see Eddie and Josh flicking tater tots at the girls' table, and I wasn't so sure that what Tommy said was true.

Maybe all this being good junk wasn't just boring for me. Maybe it was boring for Josh, too. If I wanted to go on that bike trip, I was going to have to stay out of trouble and be more fun at the same time.

CHAPTER EIGHT
Naked Presidents

After lunch on Friday, Mrs. Anderson sent me to the music room. I had to check with Mr. Cheng to see if both fourth-grade classes were having music at the same time today. We usually caused too much trouble when we were all together, but the whole fourth grade was singing a song for the assembly on the last day of school, so we had to practice. After the assembly, all the kids and parents line up in the hallways and clap while the fifth graders walk through the halls for the last time.

I think we clapped because we were supposed to be proud of them for graduating or something. But last year I heard the principal tell Mrs. Anderson that she sure was happy she'd never have to see Tommy's twin brothers again. I told Dante and Malik on the bus ride home and they cracked up.

I like being in the empty hallways, but it makes me feel like I have to be super quiet at the same time. I tiptoed up to the water fountain and took a drink. Then I walked by the other fourth-grade class and made a goofy face in the window while I waved to Josh, just to remind him I'm a fun guy. Then I went to the basement, where they keep all the music stuff. I guess that's so the classes having music won't torture the rest of the school.

Mr. Cheng wasn't there. I walked in and banged a drum while I wondered what to do. I pinged the triangle thing and pressed a few piano keys. Then I took an up-close look at the statue of the old guy's head on the top of the piano. He's Mr. Cheng's hero or something. He had creepy, blind ghost eyes and a big bow around his neck like a lady's scarf. He also had a big honker of a nose. A lot of spaghetti could come flying out of that thing. Maybe that's what the giant bow was for—to catch it.

I was about to head back to class and tell Mrs. Anderson that Mr. Cheng wasn't around, when I got an idea. A brilliant idea that would make everybody laugh and prove to Josh and Tommy that I was still fun. And the best thing—there was no way I could get caught.

I took a piece of gum out of my pocket and chewed it up really fast. Then I ripped off a piece, rolled it in a ball, and stuck it under the old guy's nose—right in booger position. The only thing that would have made it better was if my gum was green.

I was about to make a clean getaway when Mr. Cheng came in with a giant cup of coffee and a newspaper.

Uh-oh.

"Roosevelt, what are you doing in here by yourself?"

I jumped in front of the old guy. "I just got here. I just walked in, just this second," I said. "I have a hall pass," I added, waving it at him. I could feel my cheeks getting hot. I swallowed what was left of my gum so it wouldn't give me away and hoped that Tommy's brothers were lying when they said that gum comes out of your butt in a giant bubble fart if you swallow it.

"And what can I do for you?" Mr. Cheng asked.

"Mrs. Anderson wants to know if both fourth-grade classes are supposed to come to music together this afternoon," I said. "Or separately, like usual."

"Together. We're going to practice your song for the end-of-year show," he answered.

"Okay, I know all the words already!" I said, sounding way too excited. I moved my left hand onto the piano and inched it over toward the statue. "We'll all be here together, ready to sing!"

"Just not too loud, Roosevelt," Mr. Cheng said. "We want to be able to hear *all* the voices."

"President Martin Van Buren liked to sing loud," I said. "He sang so loud he drowned out everybody else at church."

"Very interesting," Mr. Cheng said. "Let's be grateful he won't be singing at our concert."

I waited for Mr. Cheng to turn away, but he kept his eyes on me.

"Millard Fillmore howls if anybody sings too loud," I said.

"Millard Fillmore?" His forehead crinkled up like he was confused.

"My dog, not the president," I said.

Mr. Cheng's eyes were still on me. My fingers grazed the edge of the statue. We weren't supposed to touch the old guy—we learned that in second grade when Zoe Richards knocked him over and he broke into a million pieces. Zoe cried and Mrs. Richards had to buy a new old guy for the piano.

"I have a dog named Millard Fillmore," I told him. "Did you know he taught himself to read using the dictionary?"

Now Mr. Cheng looked even more confused.

"The president, not the dog," I said.

"You are full of presidential facts today," Mr. Cheng said.

I just needed to walk my fingers up to the old guy's nose and remove the gum, but Mr. Cheng was still watching me.

"Did you know that President John Quincy Adams used to swim naked?" I asked.

"Is that so?"

"Yup. Every morning in the river by the White House. He just walked down there, took off his clothes, and jumped in. I don't think I'd want to see a naked president, would you?"

"No, I would not," Mr. Cheng said.

"President Taft was so big he got stuck in the bathtub in the White House and needed help getting out. He was naked, too."

I thought he might close his eyes at the idea of naked presidents, but he didn't.

"What are you going to do now?" I asked. "Read? It's silent reading time, you know."

"I think I will read," he said.

"Are you going to yell at the newspaper while you read?" I asked.

His forehead crinkled up again.

"That's what my dad does," I explained.

"Oh, no, I think I'll read quietly," he answered.

"Good. You should sit over there." I pointed to the cushy chair in the corner where Mrs. Anderson sometimes sat when we were having music. When her ears could stand it. I wanted him to turn around and look at it. "That looks like a comfortable chair."

Mr. Cheng kept his eyes on me. "Indeed it is," he said.

"Okay, then," I said.

"Roosevelt, are you trying to avoid going back to class?"

"No," I said.

"Go on, then. Mrs. Anderson will be wondering where you are."

"Okay, bye," I said, but I didn't move. I still had to

get that gum.

Mr. Cheng needed to turn his head, just for one second.

He didn't.

"Roosevelt," he said, and now he was using his mean teacher voice. If the gum didn't get me into trouble, this would.

"See you later," I said and walked to the door.

Maybe he won't see the gum, I thought. *Maybe it will dry up and fall off before silent reading time is over. And maybe, just maybe, if he does see the booger, he won't know it was me.*

CHAPTER NINE
Booger!

Both fourth-grade classes trooped down to the music room near the end of the day. Part of me hoped that the gum had fallen off, but the other part wanted everyone to know I had done something funny.

The gum was still there.

I leaned over and whispered to Tommy. "Check out the statue's nose."

He started to laugh. "Did you?"

I nodded.

Then Tommy nudged Josh. "Roosevelt put a booger on the old guy," he whispered.

Josh folded his pinky in half and pretended to be digging a wet one out of his nose. Eddie Spaghetti cracked up.

Soon you could hear the word 'booger' being whispered from kid to kid. There was lots of laughing, too. Except for Samantha Guerrero, who said "Ewwwww" really loud before she started to giggle.

Then Josh made a fake sneeze. He flicked a fake booger at Eddie, who pretended to eat it. Soon, lots of fake boogers were flying around the room.

All the while, Mr. Cheng was rearranging people in rows and telling us to pay attention. Finally we were in the order he wanted. "What's so funny?" he asked. "Settle down."

That just made everybody laugh harder.

Mr. Cheng's eyes zeroed in on me.

"Roosevelt, would you please tell me what's going on?"

I felt Tommy stiffen beside me.

"I guess everyone has colds," I said, trying to keep a straight face.

There were more giggles and another big sneeze.

"That's enough," Mr. Cheng boomed.

There was quiet for a minute. Then he started to use his mean teacher voice. "No more of this," he said. "You want this song to be perfect for the end-of-year show, don't you?"

I made sure to nod. So did a few other kids. Josh was still trying not to laugh out loud. He turned to me, and I could tell he was remembering how much fun I was before I had to be good and boring all the time.

"I'll be boogered if it's not perfect," I whispered.

Josh cracked up again. So did Eddie.

Mr. Cheng glared at them and walked over toward the piano and pounded out a few notes to get our attention. That's when he saw the booger. He eyed the statue, and then he eyed us.

Was it my imagination, or did he especially look at me?

He picked up a tissue and removed the booger. Eddie Spaghetti rubbed his upper lip and said "Ouch," sending Josh into fits of giggles again. I stared straight ahead, just in case Mr. Cheng suspected me. If he called Mom and Dad, I'd lose my new bike for sure.

The music teacher threw the tissue in the trash. "Enough of that," he said, playing the opening bars of our song. "I want you all to act like the grown-up fourth graders that you are and sing our song."

We started to sing "The Best Day of My Life." I could tell Josh and Eddie were waiting for me to sing really loud, especially for my first favorite part.

We danced with monsters through the night.

I didn't. I didn't even howl when we came to the line about howling at the moon. I wasn't going to give Mr. Cheng a reason, not one single reason, to call my parents and say I was in trouble.

I thought I was safe until it was time to go back to our classrooms.

"Roosevelt Banks, please stay behind a minute," Mr. Cheng said.

Eddie smirked and ran his finger from one side of his neck to the other. "Bye-bye, bike," he muttered.

CHAPTER TEN
A Narrow Escape

Mr. Cheng sat on the piano bench looking serious. I was trying really hard not to check out the old guy to see if the gum booger had left a mark. I saw that new bike disappear in a poof.

Then Mr. Cheng said something that shocked me so bad I almost fell over.

"Thank you, Roosevelt," he said. "I know you like to sing as loud as President Van Buren. I also know you like to howl at the moon like a wolf. Today you did neither of those things. You made your voice blend in nicely with the boys around you. Even though we started our session with a great deal of silliness," he waved his hand in the direction of the statue, "the song sounded wonderful."

Nothing about the booger?

Mr. Cheng was looking at me like he was waiting for an answer.

"You're welcome," I stammered.

"You're going to keep this up, right?" he asked. "Through the end-of-year assembly?" The way he asked it made me wonder if it was a question or a threat. Teachers could be sneaky that way.

"Right." I nodded my head really hard. "Right."

"Good," he answered. "I'm counting on you. You may go back to class now."

I breathed a big sigh of relief. I had forgotten how easy it is to get into trouble. I was lucky this time. But I had to make sure nothing like that happened again. Good thing it was Friday. I knew there was no way I'd get into trouble at home over the weekend—not with Josh and Tommy off riding their bikes.

Early Saturday morning I just happened to be looking out the front window when Josh and his dad biked toward Tommy's house. There was a big fuss when Mr. and Mrs. Wright came outside to say hi to Josh's father that included handshaking and slaps on the back and big smiles. You'd think Josh's dad was famous or something. Then Tommy wheeled his bike out from the garage and the three of them pedaled off.

I was planning to wave at them like I didn't care and had my own amazing fun and cool day planned, but they didn't even look in my direction.

Josh's dad was in the lead, riding what looked like a super fancy bike. He had a rearview mirror sticking out from his bike helmet. He raised his hand in the air and bellowed "Onward, men," like he was a general leading an army into battle or something.

"An army of jerks," I muttered.

Only I may have muttered it in a loud voice, because Mom came up behind me and put her hand on my shoulder.

"That's not very nice," she said.

"Yeah," I said. "They're a bunch of jerks."

"I meant you, Roosevelt. Your comment wasn't very nice."

"What's not nice is planning a trip for your best friends when you know one of them won't be able to go," I said.

"So make your own fun," Mom said. "How about you finish that superhero story?"

"Don't feel like it," I said, kicking the wall.

"You know Josh and Tommy aren't the only boys in the world," she said. "I could give Eddie's mom a call and see if he can come over?" she asked.

"No!" I shouted. "That noodle brain is trying to take my spot on the bike trip."

"That doesn't sound like Eddie," Mom said.

"That sounds *exactly* like Eddie," I answered.

Dad came down the stairs then, still wearing his pajamas with his hair all sticking up from bedhead.

"How about you and I have a guys-only day, buddy," he said. "I have to meet a student at the college, but afterward we can do whatever we want."

"What do you mean by whatever we want?" I asked. You had to be careful with my dad. Sometimes 'whatever we want' turned into visiting a boring old historical site or trudging through a museum.

"I don't know," he shrugged. "Lunch at the burger joint, and then maybe the baseball game. The team's having a good season," he said.

I was beginning to think the day might not be a total loss.

Before I knew it I was listening to Dad yell at some dumb guy for falling asleep in class, almost flunking history, and turning in a joke of a paper.

"My 10-year-old son could write a better paper than this," he said.

The kid slid his eyes over at me. I put my hand on my chin and thought smart things. *Ha, take that, college dude!*

Afterward we went out for super big, super messy burgers and chocolate milkshakes. Then we hit the ball field. Dad got mobbed by a bunch of boys sucking up for better grades, and I got mobbed by a bunch of girls who wanted to tell Professor Banks what a cute son he had, and everyone had to make a big deal about my name, and then Dad had to explain how his kids are named after U.S. presidents.

"Even Millard Fillmore the dog," I added.

And everyone laughed like that was the funniest thing in the world.

After that they all settled down so we could watch the game. A foul ball came flying right toward me. Without my even trying, it landed right in my hand, just like it belonged there.

Did that mean I was going to be lucky and get to go on that bike trip after all?

CHAPTER ELEVEN

Eddie Spaghetti

The next morning I sat by the window and waited for Tommy's family to get home from church. I figured he and Josh and maybe even Josh's dad would be heading out for a bike ride. I wanted to catch them before they left. Maybe Josh's dad would admire my baseball, and he'd see how cool I was and say, "This is someone we need on our trip."

Josh would tell him that I don't have a bike because it got all busted up winning Josh a blue ribbon.

Then Josh's dad would say, "Who needs to bike? We'll drive to the campground," or "Let's buy this kid a bike as a reward for the science fair," or some junk like that. And then when he said "Onward, men!" I would be one of the men.

I slipped on my baseball mitt and started throwing and catching my foul ball, enjoying the quiet *thwack* it made when it settled into the glove's pocket. Dad and I had even gotten a few of the players to autograph it.

I got to Tommy's back door just as Dante and Malik burst out of it.

"Hey, what's that?" Malik asked, plucking the ball out of my hand. He twirled it around, looking at the names. "Who are these losers?" he asked.

"Players from the college team," I said. "Not losers. They won."

He threw the ball to Dante. "Whatever, dude."

They started throwing the ball back and forth.

"Hey, I wanted to show that to Tommy. Give it back."

"He'll be out in a minute," Dante said.

He tried to get my mitt off my hand, but I pulled my arm away.

"Don't get your panties in a twist, Rosie," he said.

I was beginning to think this whole plan wasn't going to work out so good.

Tommy came out a minute later holding his bike helmet. I was chasing after his brothers, trying to get my ball back in an embarrassing game of monkey in the middle.

"Hey, Roosevelt," he said.

"I caught a foul ball at the game yesterday and my dad and I got some of the players to autograph it. It was the coolest day ever, and you could have come with us if you weren't so busy riding your bike." It came out all in a rush.

I waited for Tommy to be impressed, but he started babbling about riding with Josh's dad and how they rode *ten miles* before lunch, like that was some big huge thing. Then they ate and hung out, and biked *ten miles* back.

He walked to the garage to get his bike, talking the whole time about how cool Josh's dad was and the jokes he told and how they all drank soda after lunch and burped these really big, manly burps and how funny it was and I don't think he cared about my baseball one bit.

And then I saw something that made me feel ten times worse.

A van pulled into Tommy's driveway and Eddie Spaghetti slithered out like a snake—with his bicycle.

I looked at Tommy, waiting for an explanation, but he only looked away.

"Hey, Tommy," Eddie said. "Where's Josh?"

"He'll be here in a minute," Tommy said. His voice was quiet. His eyes landed on his brothers, still throwing my ball around.

"Roosevelt caught a fly ball at the baseball game yesterday," he said. "Players autographed it and everything."

"It was a foul ball," I mumbled. "Not a fly."

But Eddie didn't care any more than Tommy had. "How far did you bike yesterday?" he asked Tommy.

They talked about biking like I wasn't even there.

I wanted to walk away, but my legs felt like they were sinking into the earth. Dante and Malik were moving farther and farther away with my ball and I could see that it had dirt marks on it where it hit the ground—the ball I wanted to keep nice and clean because of the autographs.

Then Dante threw my baseball into Mrs. Crabapple's yard. It landed right next to the rabbit cage.

"Uh-oh," Tommy said.

Tommy's brothers tiptoed into Mrs. Crabapple's yard to pick up the ball, only at the same time they were sticking their fingers into the broken-down rabbit hutch and trying to pet the rabbits. The rabbits dashed into the enclosed part, where you couldn't see them. But Mrs. Crabapple saw Dante and Malik. She came outside yelling.

They grabbed the ball and scurried away.

"Roosevelt lost his baseball," Malik said.

"Sorry," Dante added. He tossed the ball to me,

but I wasn't expecting it and I missed the catch and it rolled down the driveway.

Eddie Spaghetti chuckled under his breath.

Mrs. Crabapple narrowed her eyes at me. "Stay away from my rabbits, or I'll talk to your mother," she said.

I nodded and felt my cheeks heating up like I was in the wrong somehow. Then I trudged in the direction of my ball, but it didn't even seem cool anymore. It looked small and dirty and sad.

Josh pedaled up. There was a tiny rear-view mirror sticking out from the side of his bicycle helmet. "Hey, Roosevelt," he said. But he didn't even wait for me to say hey back. He waved to Eddie and Tommy. "Ready?" he asked.

"Ready, dude. BDTs rule!" Eddie shouted, giving him a high five before jumping on his bike. "Let's do twenty miles like you did yesterday," he said. "Wait till you see how fast my bike goes!" His grin was so big, I thought his face was gonna crack.

Tommy rolled his eyes at me, but he still climbed onto his bike.

Josh raised his arm like his dad had yesterday. "Onward, men!" he yelled like a big jerk, and the three of them rode off.

No one said goodbye.

CHAPTER TWELVE
Frog Barf

I moped around for the rest of the day. Nothing I found to do would be as fun as riding bikes with Josh and Tommy, and every minute I was worried that Eddie was being so much fun Josh would forget all about his promise to me.

"One week down, one to go," Dad said that night with a smile.

I wasn't so sure that I had seven days before Josh caved and invited Eddie. I had to find a way to show Josh that I was just as much fun as Eddie, and I had to stay out of trouble at the same time. It's totally not fair that most of the fun things in the world are the very same things that will get a kid into trouble.

I was still thinking about that the next morning at

the bus stop. I was the first kid there, and I wanted to come up with something super funny to surprise Josh with when he arrived. And then I thought, *frogs!* Nothing's funnier than frogs.

I slid down the hill to the creek and looked around for a frog. I spotted one on the opposite creek bank. I remembered what Mom said about not getting my shoes wet, but they'd dry by after school. I tiptoed through the water until I was close to it and then— *wham!*—I trapped it in my hand.

Now all I had to do was wait for Tommy and Josh to show up and then I'd open my hand and—*bam!*— that frog would jump right in their faces.

Kid after kid came to the bus stop. Still no Tommy. Still no Josh.

Finally, I saw the two of them running down the street. That was weird. Usually they came separate. Were they having secret meetings before school now, leaving me out of one more thing?

I felt that frog wiggling in my hand and then I got

an even better idea. I popped it into my mouth. It was just a bitty thing.

Tommy and Josh were running toward me when the bus pulled up and the doors wheezed open. They raced past me, right onto the bus. And here I was with a frog on my tongue.

"Hurry it up, Roosevelt," Mrs. McKay, the bus driver, said.

I didn't know what to do. I couldn't exactly spit a frog at the bus driver. So I got on the bus.

Tommy and Josh had already fallen into their seat. I plopped down next to Eddie Spaghetti.

"You look weird," Eddie said. "Are you gonna barf?"

The spit was building up in my mouth and I was afraid to swallow. The frog didn't seem so little anymore. It felt huge—like it was growing in my mouth. And my tongue felt even huger, like it was pushing against my teeth just waiting to pop out.

I remembered what Tommy's older brothers said

about frogs and warts. Was my whole tongue going to be covered in warts? Was it really just spit in my mouth, or was that frog peeing? Or worse? It wasn't wiggling anymore. Maybe it was dead.

Now having a frog in my mouth seemed like the worst idea ever.

"Dude," Tommy said. "You are gonna barf, aren't you?"

The bus had just begun to move when I stuck out my tongue.

Suddenly that frog got all its energy back.

Tommy's mouth was a perfect round "O" of surprise when that frog shot off my tongue and onto the back of the seat he shared with Josh.

"Frog!" Josh yelled. His eyes practically bugged out when he swiped at it and missed.

The frog hopped onto Samantha Guerrero's shoulder, making her scream. "Get it off! Get it off!"

Tommy tried to help, but he was laughing so hard his whole body was shaking. His hand ended up pulling her hair instead of catching the frog, but by that time it had hopped into the window with a splat and ricocheted onto Clara Hopkins's arm.

"Ewww, gross!" she yelled, and flung it off onto William Alexander, the kid with two first names.

It landed right on top of William's head and then hopped toward the front of the bus, where kids were either trying to catch it or trying to stay away from it.

Everyone was screaming and laughing and yelling.

Josh was holding his stomach. "Dude!" he said. "You barfed a frog!"

"Ribbit, ribbit, ribbit," Eddie chanted.

The fifth graders in the back of the bus joined in: "Ribbit, ribbit, ribbit!"

One of the little kids up front was totally freaked out. "I want to go home," she wailed. Geez! You'd think she never saw a frog before.

I was too busy checking my tongue for warts and frog poop to notice that the bus had stopped. But all of a sudden everyone got really, really quiet.

Mrs. Angela was stomping down the aisle holding the frog. And let me tell you, she did not look happy. Her eyes looked like they were about to shoot lasers into my brain.

"Take this poor thing back to the creek," she said. "And hurry."

There was a long line of cars in front of and behind the bus because we had been standing still for so long. Some guy honked and then other people started honking too.

Every eye on the bus was on me as I walked behind the driver. I hopped down the bus steps and put the frog back on the creek bank.

When I got back on the bus, everyone was dead quiet.

"Hurry up back to your seat," Mrs. Angela said. "You and your friends better stay on the bus when we get to school. We're going to have a little talk with Principal Esposito."

"I better not get into trouble," Josh said to me.

"My mom's already saying that my dad can't handle three kids on a bike trip. If the principal calls her, she'll use it as an excuse to cancel. *You* brought the frog on the bus."

"You're the one who swatted it around," I answered. "Not me."

"Because a frog landed on me when I wasn't expecting it," Josh said.

I was starting to feel like I *had* swallowed the frog. And a bucketload of frog pee. If Principal Esposito called my parents, there was no way I was getting a new bike.

"I told you Roosevelt couldn't stay out of trouble for two weeks," Eddie added. He was the only one grinning.

Tommy shot me a *Dude, I'm sorry* look.

The bus pulled up to the school and the four of us sat there while the rest of the kids filed off.

The driver stood.

"Come with me, boys," she said.

CHAPTER THIRTEEN
Tommy to the Rescue

We marched into the principal's office behind the bus driver. She pointed to the troublemakers' bench. It was only big enough for three kids. Josh sat. Tommy sat next to him, but then Eddie pushed between them. I was left alone to take the chair in front of the secretary's desk.

She gave me the evil eye, looking even more than usual like she had just sucked on a sour lemon. Then she shushed Eddie, who was muttering something to Josh that I couldn't hear.

Kids were walking by, sneaking peeks and whispering on their way to class. Then the hallways quieted and I could hear the angry voice of the bus driver and the calmer rumble of Principal Esposito.

I felt like there was a bucketful of frog pee sloshing around in my stomach. How was I going to get out of this?

The bus driver walked out of the principal's office with a satisfied look. Mrs. Esposito called us into her office in time to say the Pledge of Allegiance.

Josh and Eddie stood on one side, and Tommy and I stood on the other.

"Want to explain to me why you were throwing a frog around the bus this morning?"

Eddie opened his mouth to say something, but she kept talking.

"Apparently a lot of the younger kids were scared and screaming. The driver was distracted. You could have caused a very bad accident."

I stared at my wet shoes. My cheeks were getting hot.

"So how did this happen?" Principal Esposito asked.

I could feel Josh and Eddie glaring at me, but if no one confessed, then the principal might think we were all guilty and not call any of our parents. I reminded myself that Josh was the one who swatted the frog toward the girls. All I did was spit it out.

"I expect an explanation," the principal added. "Who brought the frog on the bus? Or was it a group project?"

I kept my eyes on my shoes, but I should have known Eddie would speak up.

"I don't even have the same bus stop as them," he said. "I didn't know anything about the frog until it started hopping around."

"It wasn't me either," Josh added. "*I* didn't bring it."

"Roosevelt?" the principal asked.

I didn't say anything.

Eddie blew out a frustrated breath. "Roosevelt—"

Tommy cut him off. "It was me," Tommy said. "I brought the frog on the bus."

I stared at him, open-mouthed. Josh was doing the same thing.

"Hey—" Eddie shouted.

But Tommy just kept talking. "I saw the frog on my way to the bus stop this morning, and I wanted to show it to Mrs. Anderson—to find out exactly what kind of frog it was—and so I caught it and put in my pocket."

"And how did the frog get out of your pocket to wreak havoc on the bus?" Principal Esposito asked.

I was guessing 'wreak havoc' meant 'make girls and little kids scream.' Mrs. Esposito liked to use hard words, and when you asked her what they meant, she told you to look them up in the dictionary. It was like she took lessons from my parents or something.

Tommy opened the pocket on his jacket. "My pocket doesn't have a button or anything. I guess it opened when I sat down. And before I knew it, the frog was jumping all over the bus. I guess it was scared."

Unlike his brothers, Tommy wasn't a very good liar. He was blinking a lot and not looking the principal directly in the eye. I could see his hands were shaking a little bit. And if the principal thought about it for more than a second, she'd see that Tommy's pocket was clean and dry—no evidence that a frog had been in there.

"I'm very, very sorry," Tommy said. His voice got quiet and he sounded like he was going to cry. "Mrs. Anderson told us we should be explorers in the world, and that's what I was trying to be. I'll apologize to the driver and the whole bus after school. I just wanted to know what kind of frog it was."

The principal eyed all four of us for a minute, waiting to see if any of the rest of us had anything to say. I wondered if I should tell the truth. I thought about that new bike and how much I wanted it, and how much I wanted to go on the bike trip, and I kept my mouth shut. It's not like I asked Tommy to take the blame. He did that all by himself.

"I believe that you're sorry, Tommy," the principal said. "And I'm glad that you offered to apologize, because that's exactly what you're going to do. Instead of going to recess with the rest of your class today, I want you to write an apology to Mrs. McKay."

Tommy nodded, chewing his lips.

"The next time you're tempted to bring a frog to school, take a picture of it instead, or find a jar or a box with a lid to put it in."

"Yes, Mrs. Esposito," Tommy said. "I will."

I breathed a big sigh of relief then, because Mrs. Esposito didn't say anything about calling Tommy's parents.

"Okay," she said. "You can all go to class—quietly."

And that's when I remembered my shoes were wet from the creek. In the quiet of the office, my shoes *splooshed, squeaked* across the floor. I froze for a second, and then started to tiptoe.

I could feel my face getting hot. I was sure Mrs. Esposito could see I was guilty, but she said nothing.

Lemon Face walked us to our classrooms, so I

couldn't talk to Tommy until lunch.

"You're a good friend, Tommy, but why'd you do that?" I asked.

He shrugged. "I really want you to come on the bike trip," he said. "And you have to stay out of trouble."

"*You* could have gotten into trouble," I said. "What if Esposito called your parents?"

"Are you kidding?" Tommy asked. "After all the junk Dante and Malik have pulled, my parents would think the frog on the bus was funny. But yours—they might say you can't get that new bike."

"Josh is going to ask Eddie to go on the trip if I can't bike with you, isn't he?" I asked.

We spotted Josh and Eddie over by the fence, cracking up about something. They were just waiting for the playground monitors to look away so that they could climb it.

"Josh likes Eddie better than me," I said.

"He likes him better than me, too," Tommy said.

"Ever since Eddie found out about the trip, he's been doing everything he can to make Josh think he's awesome at everything. He tries to leave me out of things, too, so he can be buddy-buddy with Josh."

"I wouldn't be surprised if he tries to get me in trouble so he can go," I said.

Tommy nodded. "If you want that bike, you're going to have to stay away from Eddie Spaghetti."

CHAPTER FOURTEEN

Eddie's Secret

I knew how close I had come to losing that bike on the bus, so I tried *really* hard to stay out of trouble for the next few days. Mostly that meant staying as far away from Eddie Spaghetti as I could.

Then I had just three days to go before bike day.

"I know I'm not supposed to get my new bike until Monday, but all the best yard sales are on Saturday," I said. "So can we get up super early on Saturday and look?" I asked. "I promise not to ride it until Monday.

"We have to get to the yard sales early, early, early," I added. "Before the best bikes are gone."

Dad scratched his head. "Maybe we should give it another week."

Mom nodded. "I really enjoy this good kid we have on our hands now. I think another week might be just the thing to make sure it sticks."

My stomach sank. There was no way Josh would wait another week before inviting Eddie in my place. "I've been good for almost two whole weeks. A deal's a deal. That's what you always say. And we have a deal."

Dad chuckled. "I'm just teasing, buddy. You're right. A deal's a deal. We'll get up early Saturday morning and see what we can find."

"We're going to find the best bike ever. I know it!" I said.

"But first you have two more days to be good. And we expect this good behavior to last even after you get your bike," Mom said. "You can't stop cleaning up the yard just because there's nothing on the line."

"No problem," I said. "I'll keep it up."

I was feeling good Friday morning until Mom sprang it on me.

"Eddie's going to get off the bus with you this afternoon," she said. "I arranged a play date."

"A play date—with Eddie Spaghetti?"

"Oh, excuse me," Mom said. "A *hang-out*."

"Mom, how could you do that without asking me? Eddie's a zombie noodle brain. He's totally trying to steal my spot in the bike trip. Josh is hardly talking to me anymore because of Eddie."

Mom looked me in the eye. She had on her serious expression. The one that said, 'Listen, Roosevelt,' without her actually having to say the words.

"Eddie's mom told me a secret about Eddie, and you can't let him know I told you. And you can't tell your other friends."

"Does he have some kind of zombie disease?"

"What in the world would make you think that?" Mom asked.

"He had a zombie birthday party. And once he

said that Emily Park smelled like a dead zombie and she cried."

"This secret has nothing to do with zombies," Mom said. "Now remember, this is just between you and me."

"And Eddie's mom."

"Yes," Mom nodded. "And Eddie's mom."

"And Eddie," I said.

"Yes, and Eddie."

I could tell Mom wanted to spill the secret already, so I didn't point out that four people was a lot when it came to secrets.

"You and Eddie used to play together a lot more than you do now, and he misses you. He doesn't have kids his age who live on his street like you do. He's sad that he doesn't have a best friend. He used to think of you as his best friend."

"Eddie has lots of friends," I said. "Everyone likes him. All the guys in fourth grade went to his birthday party even though he told everyone the cake was going to be zombie brains."

"Yes, but he doesn't have best friends like you do to play with every day after school. He's never the one special friend who gets invited to sleepovers or to go on camping trips."

I never knew that Eddie used to think I was his best friend. I thought he didn't have a best friend because he didn't want one. Tommy was always my BF, so I don't even know where Eddie got *that* idea.

"I can't help it if Josh's dad says that he can only invite two friends," I said. "I don't want Eddie to go in my place."

"I'm sure Eddie doesn't want to go in your place. He wants to go *with* you," Mom said. "Can you try to include him more?"

I felt sad and left out when Josh and Tommy rode off on their bikes without me. I guess Eddie felt like that a lot. I told Mom I'd try, but in my head I knew I'd wait until *after* I got my new bike. I still didn't trust him.

"He's going to try to get me into trouble," I grumbled.

"Roosevelt, Eddie can't get you into trouble unless you let him," Mom answered.

CHAPTER FIFTEEN

Crash!

I worried all day about what kind of trouble Eddie Spaghetti could get me into. I felt even more worried when I found out that Josh had a dentist appointment and couldn't ride bikes, so Tommy was going to hang out with us after school, too. What if Eddie managed to get both Tommy and me kicked off the camping trip?

"What's the farthest you've gone?" Eddie asked Tommy on the bus ride home.

"We did twenty-five miles on Saturday," Tommy said. "We stopped for lunch halfway."

"Wow," I said. "You're almost ready. You'll do another five miles easy."

"You'll be ready, too. Don't worry," Tommy said to

me. "What kind of bike are you going to get?"

Eddie pretended to look out the window like he didn't care, but I remembered what Mom had said and felt a little bad. I was learning what it was like to feel left out.

I shrugged. "My dad and I are going to a bunch of yard sales on Saturday."

"You'll find a great one," Tommy said.

"A *used* bike?" Eddie said really loud, making other kids on the bus turn and look at us. I felt my cheeks getting hot.

"It'll be a disgusting pile of junk," he said. "You won't be able to keep up. My bike is new and super fast."

I didn't say anything. I was just glad Josh wasn't on the bus to hear that.

"It'll be a *great* bike," Tommy said.

Eddie snorted, but Tommy looked at me and rolled his eyes. He was a good friend.

The three of us jumped off the bus when we got

to our stop and walked down the street. We told
Tommy we'd call for him when we were ready to
hang out. Eddie seemed kind of quiet, and I started
to think I might get through this afternoon without
getting into trouble after all.

Fillmore bounded up to us when I opened the
door, sniffing and licking and wagging his tail. Mom
was right behind him.

"Hi, boys," she said. "How was school?"

"Okay," I said.

"Awesome," Eddie answered. "I learned tons and
tons and tons of stuff."

"That's great," Mom said. "How do the two of
you feel about taking Fillmore for a W-A-L-K after
you've had a snack? He's missed them."

"Okay," I said. Fillmore loved walks, but I wasn't
allowed to walk him around the neighborhood by
myself, or just me and Kennedy. Josh and Tommy
had been so busy riding bikes that the poor pup had
to settle for running around in the backyard. It wasn't

as much fun for him as being able to sniff around the whole neighborhood and pee on everyone's bushes.

A few cookies and a couple of bananas later, I got Fillmore's leash and we headed for Tommy's house. Fillmore trotted in front, wagging his tail and trying to pull me to go faster, especially when he saw a squirrel. That dog was crazy for squirrels. I don't even want to think about what he'd do if he ever caught one.

Tommy joined us and we made one loop around the block, half running and half walking. Fillmore almost pulled the leash out of my hand once when he saw a chipmunk, but I held on. We were singing our fourth-grade song and howling whenever we came to the line about howling at the moon. Fillmore joined in with a howl of his own and we totally cracked up.

We were about to start a second loop around the block when Eddie Spaghetti pointed to the rabbit hutch in Mrs. Crabapple's yard.

"Let's go see the rabbits," he said.

"No way," I told him. "You saw how she acted on Sunday, and all Tommy's brothers did was go after my baseball."

"Once she caught Dante and Malik playing with her rabbits. She grabbed their ears and marched them over to our back door. She wouldn't leave until she made sure they'd be in trouble."

"Big trouble?" Eddie asked, his eyes dancing.

"Big trouble," Tommy said. "They weren't allowed to watch TV or play video games for a whole week."

"That's only because they got caught. I bet we could go in there and pet those rabbits and she'd never even know."

I was getting a bad feeling. "She keeps a lock on the hutch now," I said. "So you can't even get the rabbits out. And her car's in the driveway."

Eddie stared right into my eyes. "I dare you."

I'm normally the kind of guy that doesn't walk away from a dare, but I had a new bike on the line and Eddie knew it. "I'm not doing it."

Eddie Spaghetti didn't want to take no for an answer. He pointed toward the rabbits with an evil grin and shouted, "Squirrel!"

Eddie took off running. Fillmore followed, tugging his leash right out of my hand.

Eddie turned around and ran backwards, trying to get Fillmore to catch up with him. He wasn't watching where he was going.

What happened next seemed like it happened in slow motion, but I know it happened really fast. It was like my brain was taking pictures so I'd remember every horrible second.

BANG! Eddie banged into the rabbit hutch.

WOOF! Fillmore jumped on top of Eddie, putting his front paws on Eddie's chest. I think maybe Fillmore was trying to protect Eddie, but Eddie fell backwards.

That's when everything went really, really wrong.

SHAKE! The hutch wobbled on its shaky legs while the three rabbits inside dashed into the closed part, where I couldn't see them.

CRASH! The hutch fell backward with a crash.

CRACK! The roof cracked in half.

THUMP! Half of the roof fell right off into the too-tall grass.

HOP! Three terrified bunnies hopped right out of that hutch and into the too-tall grass.

BARK! Fillmore took off after those bunnies, barking his head off. The only thing I could do was race after him.

KICK! I was running so fast that I kicked Eddie Spaghetti right in the head when I dashed by.

SCREECH! I was way at the back of the yard behind an overgrown bush when I heard Mrs. Crabapple's back door screech open. I'm not allowed to say the words that were coming out of her mouth, but let me tell you—they were loud.

CHAPTER SIXTEEN
Trouble–Big Trouble

Fillmore quieted down when we got to the creek. He splashed in the water while I strained to hear what Mrs. Crabapple was saying—after she stopped yelling bad words.

Tommy and Eddie were both trying to tell her it was an accident.

I felt bad that they were getting the blame, when it was partly Fillmore's fault. If he hadn't jumped on Eddie, the hutch wouldn't have fallen over. With a new bike on the line, I wasn't going to confess. I figured Tommy would be okay.

Mrs. Crabapple was more than mad, though— she was scared out of her mind.

"They won't survive," she cried. "Don't you

understand? A bigger animal could come along and eat them. They're pets. They don't know how to protect themselves."

"We'll find them," I heard Tommy promise in a high, scared voice.

Eddie took up the search right away. "Here, bunnies," he said. "Here, bunnies."

I could hear the three of them moving through the grass, trying to find the rabbits. I crouched where I was, shaking, hoping Fillmore wouldn't give me away. I knew that once those rabbits were found, Mrs. Crabapple was going to do to Tommy and Eddie what she had done to Dante and Malik—make sure they were punished.

I heard a quiet woof behind me and some heavy-duty sniffing. Fillmore had one of the rabbits cornered between the bush and the creek. I had to get there before he decided to find out what rabbit tasted like, but if I ran, he might chomp and run. I tiptoed over and scooped up the trembling bunny, making a kind of kangaroo pocket with my T-shirt. Then I grabbed Fillmore's leash and double-wrapped it around my hand. He wasn't getting away again.

I was wondering how to return the rabbit to Mrs. Crabapple without getting into trouble when I heard Tommy yell, "Found one!"

"That's Peter. Give him to me," Mrs. Crabapple said.

I heard the rabbit hutch being lifted. I guess they were trying to put it back together.

"Keep looking. Keep looking," Mrs. Crabapple said. "We have to find Benjamin and Flopsy." She sounded like she was going to cry.

There was a row of hedges between Mrs. Crabapple's yard and the O'Connors'—the neighbors on the opposite side of her house from Tommy's—chain-link fence. The fence kept the O'Connors' Dobermans, Trigger and Bullet, in their own yard. Just my luck— both killer dogs were outside.

I crouched between the hedge and the fence for

a second, feeling Benjamin or Flopsy shake against my belly. It wasn't as bad as a frog in my mouth, but I was a little afraid of what might come out of that rabbit while it was in there. And then it did. Yuck.

Rabbit number two was found. "Benjamin," Mrs. Crabapple yelled.

I could hear her moving in my direction, telling the boys to keep their eyes open.

If I let Flopsy go, would she hop in the right direction, or would she end up as Doberman dinner?

I couldn't risk that, but I didn't want to risk my new bike either.

Slowly and quietly, I crept between the hedges and the fence, hoping that no one would look there. Fillmore trotted next to me like he was the most innocent dog in the world. The Dobermans didn't interest him.

I couldn't say the same for Trigger and Bullet. I'm not sure if it was me, or Fillmore, or Flopsy, but they started barking like crazy.

Mrs. Crabapple screamed so loud that I heard her over the barking.

"Those killer dogs have my Flopsy! Those killer dogs have my Flopsy!"

No more creeping for me. I ran. I made it to the street just before she got to the line of hedges. Tommy and Eddie were on her heels. Even from a distance I could see that they looked scared.

I walked to the front of Mrs. Crabapple's house and then into her yard.

"Mrs. Crawford," I called in an innocent voice. "I think I have one of your rabbits."

She burst out from behind the hedges. Tommy and Eddie were right behind her. I opened my T-shirt.

"Flopsy!" She snatched her up and kissed her on the nose. "Thank goodness you found her," she said.

"She was hopping around your front yard," I said. I opened my eyes extra wide so that she could see I was being honest. Fillmore wagged his tail like the most innocent dog in the world.

Behind Mrs. Crabapple, Eddie narrowed his eyes at me.

I raised my hands, palms up. What was I supposed to do? Step up and take the blame? It was Eddie's fault, mostly. And a little bit Fillmore's.

The three of us and Fillmore started to edge our way backward while Mrs. Crabapple settled Flopsy in the hutch, which was even more wobbly than before. One big bunny hop and that thing would fall apart.

We weren't even to the sidewalk yet when Mrs. Crabapple turned on her heel and announced that she was going to have a talk with Tommy's parents. She stopped to glare at Eddie Spaghetti. "And you, young man. I don't know you, but believe you me, your parents will be informed."

"I only helped find them," Tommy protested.

But Mrs. Crabapple didn't listen. She grabbed his arm and marched toward his house.

Tommy had no choice but to follow. He looked

over his shoulder at me, but what was I supposed to do? Mrs. Crabapple wouldn't have listened to me either. And I had a new bike on the line.

She was knocking on Tommy's door before Eddie, Fillmore, and I even reached my house. I led Eddie into the backyard.

"Nice, Roosevelt," Eddie said with a sneer. "Let Tommy take the blame again. What kind of friend are you?"

"What? You're the one who started it." I whispered so Mom wouldn't hear. "*You* made Fillmore follow you into the Crabapples' yard. *You* fell back against the rabbit hutch. Why should I take the blame for that?"

"It's not my fault you're too weak to hold onto your dog. Fillmore caused all the trouble," Eddie said. "And now Tommy's going to get punished. But I guess bikes are more important than people to you."

"You're a liar," I said. "You started all that because

you're trying to steal my spot on the bike trip. Don't think I don't know. You only get to go if I don't— because no one really wants you."

Eddie's face went pale and I could see that he was gritting his teeth. But at the same time his eyes were suddenly wet, because maybe he thought what I said was true. I immediately started to feel bad, but I was still mad, too.

We were glaring at each other when Mom called us into the house. Mrs. Crabapple had talked to Tommy's mom, who called my mom, who called Eddie's mom, who called Mrs. Crabapple.

No one even talked to us about what happened. There was a flurry of phone calls, and everyone decided that Tommy and Eddie would have to pay to have the rabbit hutch replaced. Tommy's father wanted to build one for her. Dante and Malik were already trying to figure out how to make a bunny penthouse and an elevator, but she insisted on a super nice one from a store. She had a picture of it all ready to give them, like she had been wanting this one for a while. Tommy and Eddie were going to have to split the cost, and it was expensive. They were also going to have to do yard work for Mrs. Crabapple. That wasn't going to be fun.

I asked my mom about Tommy and the bike trip. "I don't know, buddy," she said. "If he has to spend the next few weekends working in Mrs. Crawford's yard, he won't able to go."

Eddie narrowed his eyes and gave me a look that said, *What kind of friend are you?* I waited for him to tell Mom about my part in the great rabbit escape, but he didn't. We barely said two words to each other before his mom came to pick him up.

I wanted to call Tommy, but I didn't know what to say. Why didn't he tell on me?

"I'm glad you had the good sense to stay out of Mrs. Crawford's yard," Mom said to me over dinner. "Where were you when it happened?"

"Up the block with Millard Fillmore," I mumbled,

moving the food around on my plate.

Fillmore thumped his tail, like he was agreeing with me.

"Lucky you came back in time to find the last rabbit," Dad said. "I don't trust those Dobermans."

I nodded, trying to force my throat to swallow a bite of mashed potatoes.

"Mrs. Crawford loves those bunnies," Mom added. "She rescues rabbits every year after Easter. People get them for Easter presents, and when they realize how much work they are, they either just let them go or bring them to an animal shelter."

"They do?" I asked. "That's messed up."

Mom nodded. "Mrs. Crawford pays to have them neutered so that they can't have babies. Then she tries to find good homes for them. When she can't find anyone to take them, she keeps them. Sometimes she has as many as ten rabbits at a time. It's expensive for her."

"I want a bunny," Kennedy announced. "I want

TEN bunnies."

"Maybe when you're older, sweetie," Dad said.

I was feeling worse and worse. Not only was Mrs. Crabapple some kind of bunny superhero, Tommy was in major trouble. And it wasn't *all* Eddie's fault. Some of it was Fillmore's. And maybe mine, too. If I had held on to him better, he might not have jumped on Eddie and sent the hutch flying.

If I confessed, I'd lose out on my new bike and the trip. If I didn't, I'd be the worst friend who ever lived.

"May I be excused?" I asked. "I'm not very hungry."

Mom reached over to feel my forehead, the way moms do. "No fever," she said. "Go ahead. I'll be in in a little while."

CHAPTER SIXTEEN
A Deal's a Deal

About an hour later, Mom and Dad came into my room. Mom sat on the edge of the bed and Dad took the desk chair with no wheels like always. "You didn't get into trouble with Tommy and Eddie," Mom said. "I'm sure it took some courage on your part to hold back instead of joining in with your friends."

"I'm proud of you, buddy," Dad said. He stood up and stretched. "In fact, a deal's a deal—"

"I don't deserve a new bike!"

Then words tumbled out and ran all over the place just like those bunnies in the grass. "It was me. It was Fillmore, I mean. I did it by accident. Eddie started it and then Fillmore ran in after him and jumped and they knocked over the hutch. But I didn't have a good hold on the leash, which is stupid because he chases everything, and Eddie didn't want me to get a bike and so he started it. And I pretended to be a big hero and find the rabbit when it's partly my fault they got lost in the first place. I'm the worst friend in the whole world because Tommy's the best friend in the whole world even when the principal is talking to you about frogs and bus accidents and he shouldn't be in trouble. I don't deserve to go on a bike trip or have any friends and no one will want to be my friend ever again anyway."

Dad and Mom were both really quiet until I finished. Then Mom got me to tell the story again but slower. It was easier this time, because I wasn't crying so hard. I left out the part about the frog on the bus, but I told them everything about the rabbits, beginning with Eddie daring me to go into the yard and Fillmore chasing him in. And the worst part was the one about me letting Tommy get into trouble when he didn't do anything.

"I don't deserve a new bike," I said. "A deal's a deal."

Mom smoothed my hair over my forehead. "I'm glad you told us the truth," she said. "Do you feel better?"

I nodded, but I didn't really. In one way I did, because I wasn't the worst friend in the world anymore. All Tommy did was try to find the rabbits, and now he wouldn't be in trouble anymore. But I felt worse because there was no way I was going on the bike trip now. Josh and Tommy would be two best friends and I'd be bouncing from group to group like Eddie Spaghetti, hoping someone would include me. And maybe no one would after hearing about what a horrible friend I was to Tommy.

"We'll call Tommy's parents and tell them the whole story," Dad said. "And you and Eddie will have to share the cost of the hutch and do yard work for Mrs. Crawford."

"We'll talk about everything else in the morning," Mom said. "Think you can go to sleep?"

"I'll try," I said.

I listened to their voices murmuring into their phones and to each other. I was pretty sure I heard my dad say, "A deal's a deal," right before I fell asleep.

CHAPTER SEVENTEEN
Onward, Men

Two weeks later I woke up super early. My clothes were ready—Mom had bought me a cool, new bike helmet—and all I had to do was put my lunch in my backpack.

Mom and Dad waited for me in the kitchen. They were sleepy-eyed but excited. I put my backpack and my new bike helmet on the table and gave Mom a big hug.

"Thanks for saying I could go," I said.

"You earned it," she answered. "All that work you did in Mrs. Crawford's yard, and organizing a fundraiser at school to help her pay for the rabbits. But don't forget to be good just because you have your new bike. You can't suddenly turn into a bad boy."

I wiggled my eyebrows at her. "Not even a little bit?"

Dad wiggled his, too. "Yeah, Mom, not even a little bit?"

She laughed. "Not even a little bit."

After I had done all that stuff for Mrs. Crawford, I learned what Dad really meant by 'a deal's a deal.'

He had already bought a new bike from a neighbor of Aunt Jessica's. It was too late to go back on *that* deal, even though I wasn't perfectly good. And Mrs. Crawford was so happy with all the yard work Eddie and I did. And with the promise of a fundraiser, she told Tommy's dad he could build a new rabbit hutch if he really wanted to. He loved that kind of stuff, and he got Dante and Malik to help. It was the fanciest rabbit hutch anyone had ever seen.

Eddie and I had to promise to help Mrs. C—we stopped calling her Crabapple because she wasn't really crabby once you got to know her—feed her rabbits and give them water and to never, ever, ever let them out of the hutch. And Eddie was less of a troublemaker because he got to come over and play a couple of afternoons a week and on weekends. Josh and Tommy liked to help, and we were kinda, sorta turning into four best friends.

I ate my cereal really fast and then it was time to go. Tommy was waiting for Dad and me in his driveway, and the three of us climbed on our bikes and set off for the old railroad trail.

Josh and his dad were at the trailhead. The dads started shifting things around in the bike trailers, spreading the weight. We were ready to go when Eddie Spaghetti's mom drove up and he bounced out of the van with his bike.

Yup, Eddie was coming—and so was Dad. That's how I fixed it. Josh's dad said Eddie could come if another dad came along. Eddie wasn't a bad kid, really, he just wanted to have a best friend. And since I have the best dad in the world, he said he'd come. I even got him to promise not to tell us about how many presidents rode bikes. I didn't know until later that I should have asked him not to tell us about presidents who went camping, too.

"Ready, buddy?" Dad asked.

"Ready," I answered.

We watched Josh and his dad climb on their bikes and start to pedal.

"Onward, men!" they shouted.

Tommy and Eddie were next.

Dad and I were right behind them.

I was so happy I started to sing. I sang as loud as President Van Buren, especially when I got to my favorite line.

We danced with monsters through the night.

Josh, Tommy, and Eddie all joined in. Even the dads knew the words.

We weren't just singing the song, we were living it. It was "The Best Day of My Life."

ABOUT THE AUTHOR

Laurie Calkhoven grew up in a neighborhood very much like Roosevelt's, and she's always been interested in wacky presidential facts. She's never swallowed a frog, knocked over a rabbit hutch, or sung too loud in music class, but she is the author of many books for young readers. Laurie now lives and works in New York City.